J
E
RAS

Raschka,
Christopher.

The blushful
hippopotamus.

$14.95

DATE			
		JUN 1 9 1997	
APR 1 4 1997			
		JUL 3 1997	
MAY 0 7 1997			
MAY 1 5 1997		JUL 2 0 1997	
MAY 2 9 1997		AUG 1 3 1997	
		SEP 0 8 1997	
DEC 1 1997		SEP 2 9 1997	

BAKER & TAYLOR

the Blushful Hippopotamus

Chris Raschka

Orchard Books New York

Orchard Books • 95 Madison Avenue • New York, NY 10016

Manufactured in the United States of America
Printed by Barton Press, Inc.
Bound by Horowitz/Rae
Book design by Chris Raschka
The text of this book is hand lettered.
The illustrations are watercolor with india ink and oil sticks.

1 2 3 4 5 6 7 8 9 10

Library of Congress Cataloging-in-Publication Data
Raschka, Christopher.
The blushful hippopotamus / Chris Raschka.
p.   cm.
"A Richard Jackson book"—Half t.p.
Summary: Though Roosevelt the hippopotamus's sister teases him
because he blushes a lot, his best friend helps him feel better
about himself.
ISBN 0-531-09532-0. — ISBN 0-531-08882-0 (lib. bdg.)
[1. Hippopotamus—Fiction.   2. Brothers and sisters—Fiction.
3. Blushing—Fiction.]   I. Title.
PZ7.R18148Bl   1996   [E]—dc20   95-51562

for B.F.T.

I am the blushful hippopotamus

or so my sister sometimes calls me now.

If I fall down, she likes to call me that.

Darn that sister! She makes me mad, you know.

She says, "Roosevelt" (yes, this is my name),

"are you blushing again, baby brother?"

She says this when I'm eating an ice cream

with my friend Lombard, my best friend, Lombard.

"You are a blushful hippopotamus!"

she says, when I'm just having a little

trouble with my bike.

"Are you blushing again, baby brother?"

3?

she asks, when I'm working on my counting.

She says "You are a blushful hippo baby!"

Buggalo?

Buffalo!

when I'm trying to think of the right name.

Darn that sister!

"Lombard, <u>am</u> I a blushful hippopotamus?"

Lombard says,

"Roosevelt, a hopeful hippopotamus
is what you are."

Lombard says,

"A mindful hippopotamus,
this is you, too."

My friend says,

"A thoughtful hippopotamus
is who is you."

And he says,

"A skillful hippopotamus
is what it is you are."

Lombard says,

"A wonderful hippopotamus
are you, are you, are you!"

"Thank you, Lombard."